Trouble in Treeville

Shirley Santilli

by **Shirley Santilli**

with illustrations by **Lorrie Santilli Wolfinger**

Lorrie Santilli Wolfinger

2014

To our grandchildren, great-grandchildren,
and children of all ages everywhere.

W elcome to Treeville, the town above your head.

The home of our feathered friends, where baby birds are fed.

The bluejays are policemen that fly from tree to tree.
The bluejays must protect the birds, like police watch you and me.

The birds all live together as happy as can be,
Among the pines and maples, and the apple trees.

Into their lives came trouble. It was an awful pill.
The bluejays, they found trouble, such trouble in Treeville.

Judge Oliver Owl was sleeping in his office in the tree.

The sparrows on the East Side...

...were as busy as could be.

Lord Baltimore Oriole in Pinetree Heights
was feeding on a worm.

The mother robin to her children
was being very firm.

But, poor Mrs. Hummingbird was given quite a scare.
She had left her nest for lunch, leaving four eggs there.

Upon her return to her nest she had to be revived.

For in her nest lay not four eggs...

Now there were five!

The bluejay, he came on the wing.
What happened here was a terrible thing!

The cardinal in the tree nearby
was asked to come and testify.

18

"What did you see?" the bluejay said.

The cardinal replied, "I was still in bed."

The martin from the apartment house said,

"Why don't you go ask my spouse?"

$\mathbf{M}$rs. Martin was questioned:

"Tell me, what did you see?"

The martin replied, "A cowbird I spied,
After Mrs. Hummingbird left the tree."

"Ah," said the bluejay, "A cowbird you did spy.
I'll go and question Mrs. Wren to see if she flew by."

Mrs. Wren was busy cleaning her house.
"I didn't see a cowbird, but I did see a mouse."

So on to Apple Valley Officer Bluejay flew,
And inquired of the woodpecker,
"Have you seen a cowbird? Well, have you?"

The woodpecker thought before she spoke.
The cowbird again—this was no joke.

27

The cowbird was being a terrible pest.
She was laying eggs in another bird's nest.

It was only the year before,
in the woodpecker's nest the cowbird lay four!

Now from the oak tree the blackbirds flew.

"The flicker has cornered the cowbird! It's true!"

"Go get the owl!" The bluejay said.

So they got Judge Oliver out of bed.

They all flew down to the old oak tree
To see the cowbird in her misery.

T here was the cowbird trapped in the tree.

The flicker was as proud as could be.

35

"You've done it again!" Judge Oliver raged.

"Now you must go in the people's cage."

36

"Out of Treeville you must go,
to live one year in the cage below.
To lay your eggs, and not to go.
To stay and watch your family grow."

37

So now in Treeville there is peace...

Until the cowbird is released.

Shirley Santilli was born in Mohrsville, Pennsylvania in 1934. She currently lives in Shoemakersville, where she has resided for fifty-eight years. She worked as a telephone operator and in the local school library, and was on the school board for twenty years. She was also the secretary for her husband, John, in his business, San-Tool. Shirley and John are the proud heads of a family of three daughters, six grandchildren, and four great-grandchildren. Her family inspired many of the stories she's written. All of her children and grandchildren have fond memories of listening to her storytelling when they were young. She wrote *Trouble in Treeville* in the 1960s, but it wasn't until 2011 that she decided to finally pursue publication. With her daughter, Lorrie, as illustrator, Shirley's longtime dream of becoming a published author finally became a reality!

Lorrie Santilli Wolfinger was born in Reading, Pennsylvania in 1956. She currently resides in Shoemakersville in the home next to her parents' home where she grew up. Lorrie and her husband, Thomas, have three children and four grandchildren. Currently she is an elementary physical education teacher, but she has also worked in a bookstore and as an acrobatics instructor at several dance studios. Her artwork has been admired as set designs for annual dance reviews and Nutcracker performances. Lorrie has always loved children's books and playing with children. Illustrating *Trouble in Treeville* and working with her mother is one of her proudest accomplishments. It is a dream come true!

CPSIA information can be obtained
at www.ICGtesting.com
Printed in the USA
LVXC02n1021191213
366038LV00002B/4